DEBORAH MCTIERNAN

A Mystery's Collection of 101 Love Spells,

From the Diary of Shellaire Lombard

First published by Actual Magic Enterprises, LLC 2020

An Actual Magic Enterprises Press Book, published by Lightning Source, a subsidiary of Ingram Press Publishers. Actual Magic Enterprises Press Books are available through Ingram Press, for order through Ingram Press Catalogues, Barnes & Noble, Amazon, and KDP.

Library of Congress cataloging-in-publication data

McTiernan, Deborah, 1956-

A Mystery's Collection of 101 Love Spells, from Shellaire Lombard's Diary, And the Magical World of Lilly Noble: a novel/ by Deborah McTiernan. —— 1sted. P. Cm.

Summary: A collection of 101 original love spells written for young mystics and mysterys around the world. Popular entertainment for bedtime reading, slumber parties, and sleepovers, with no guarantee of real boyfriend results. Novels from the Magical World of Lilly Noble build courage, confidence, and self-esteem in young magical folk by countering the darkness in others with kindness, patience, and understanding.

Library of Congress Control Number: 2020912286

Printed in the United States of America

First Printing: October 2020

Actual Magic Enterprises, L.L.C.

www.deborahmctiernan.com

First edition

ISBN: 978-1-7353558-0-1

This book was professionally typeset on Reedsy.
Find out more at reedsy.com

For my fans,
Thank you for bringing your special brand of magic into my life.

Dear Mystics & Mysterys,

May the Elements of Magic attract your heart's desire.

Warmest regards,

DEBORAH MCTIERNAN

Contents

Foreword

I was deeply touched when Shellaire Lombard asked me to write the forward for this very special edition of A MYSTERY'S COLLECTION OF 101 LOVE SPELLS. These incantations, amulets, and potions were taken from entries in her daily diary and her own personal BOOK OF SHADOWS.

Culled from Shellaire's collection of her very best spells and charms, within these pages you will discover excellent ways to banish pesky gossip, craft beads from rose petals, and enchant dolls from mere paper.

It is Shellaire's sincere hope that A MYSTERY'S COLLECTIONS OF 101 LOVE SPELLS will unite mortals and magical folk in harnessing the happy gifts of love and imagination.

All that remains is for me to warn you; words are powerful magic. But it's the intentions beneath your words that set magic in motion. If your intentions are good, what you create with your magic will bring love and joy into the world. And, if your intentions are evil, well you get the picture.

Your real thoughts are always revealed in the results of your incantations. So remember, what you put out to others will always return to you. Believe good things about yourself and others and you will wield a special brand of magic far beyond the powers of any mystic or mystery.

Madam Lucrezia Saboulia currently teaches POWER OF IN-TENTIONS at Bonaventure's Academy of Magic located on Raven's Landing, Maine.

Best Wishes,
Madam Lucrezia Saboulia

THIS BOOK BELONGS TO

_____

1

Actual Magic 101

White Magic Versus Black Isn't as Big a Deal as People Think

Here's the difference: With white magic, spells are cast with no particular person in mind. When you cast a spell with someone in mind, this is considered black magic because you are trying to directly influence someone's emotions. But, even when casting a white magic spell, in the end, someone (usually the right person) will be influenced.

So, work your spells carefully. And remember, what you do will eventually come back to you.

* * *

A List of Common Love Spell Supplies

When performing love spells, the best plan is to have everything you need organized in front of you before you cast.

Here is a list of some of the basic items:

Magic Spell Box: A place to stash your spells so they will be undisturbed after being cast. Your Magic Spell Box can be as simple as a shoe or hat box you've decorated yourself, an old jewelry box, or treasure chest. The choice is yours.

Stones: Rose Quartz, Amethyst, Lapis Lazuli, Red Jasper. It's okay if these stones are set in jewelry. They will still work.

Flowers: Rose petals, Lavender, honeysuckle, chamomile (you can substitute this one with tea bags)

Oils and herbs: Look in the kitchen spice rack.

Candles in pink, white, or red.

Most of the supplies used for the spells in this book can be purchased at your neighborhood Dollar Store.

* * *

How to Cast Love Spells - With a Warning

Here are a few things to keep in mind when casting any spell. But love spells in particular carry an element of risk, and can be very tricky. First of all, understand why you are casting your chosen spell. This is probably the most important aspect of spell casting. Ask yourself a few simple questions before you begin:

Is your spell directed at a specific person?

Are you attempting to manipulate someone's feelings? (For

personal gain, perhaps? Or, to get back at someone?)

Are you casting your spell to get someone's attention? (Getting someone to notice you, depending on your motives. This can be considered personal gain.)

Here's the warning part I mentioned at the top of this page:

Casting spells to cause specific emotions in someone that aren't already inside them, or using magic to lure someone away from someone else will bring nothing but trouble your way.

I guarantee it!

But if your spells come from a pure wish to attract true love, your chances of success at finding your heart's desire tip heavily in your favor.

Leave your heart (and your mind) open.

Remember, your magic will bring to you exactly what you need, at exactly the right time.

Simplest Love Spell Ever Written
I promise to cherish.
I promise to be true.
Send love my way.
Today will do.

* * *

Adding Elements to Your Love Spells

Elements are not always needed to insure a spell's success.

But they do help by focusing the spell caster's attention and intentions while writing and casting an enchantment.

And again, with elements, as with spells, keep your ingredients simple.

Use your imagination. Don't go in search of a genuine eye of newt, or tongue of frog, when a simple substitution of a small black bead (for the newt's eye), or fabric tongue (for the frog) is all that's needed. Magic begins and ends with your true intentions. The rest is ceremony. Using substitutions are a lot less icky, and the newt and frog will thank you!

Here's a more detailed list of elements to keep on hand:

Candles: pink, red, and white for love spells

Ribbon, yarn, or thread (used for binding and sewing charms): red, pink, and white

Fabric: have swatches available in red, pink, and white

Herbs & Spices: Cinnamon, cloves, vanilla beans (or extract), roses, and lavender

Gems Stones: Rubies (most powerful love gem), garnets, red jasper, red jade, and pearls

Photographs (or a copy of a photograph) of your intended heart's desire

Paper and confetti hearts, sequins, and beads

This is your spell, so get busy and use your imagination!

* * *

How to Write Your Own Spells

Homemade spells are powerful magic when you craft an enchantment with a specific purpose in mind. Your own words combine with your energy making the magic personal.

Okay, I get it if the idea of writing your own spells sounds overwhelming and a little bit scary. It did to me at first, too. But, Madam Saboulia taught us that whipping up our own enchantments is as simple as writing short poems. And remember, when you write your own spells, the magic cast is real. Trust me. I know this stuff.

To begin, simply think about what it is you wish to accomplish with your spell. Since this book is all about love spells, let's begin there. Spells don't require a lot of words, but every word you choose has to serve a purpose.

Crafting the spell is as easy as writing a two or four line poem, or borrowing lyrics from a favorite song. Keep your spell simple and try to make it rhyme, (though this is not a must) and be specific about what you really want.

Here's a quick (and familiar) example:

Love Star Spell

Star light, star bright,
First star I see tonight.
I wish I may, I wish I might,
Have this wish I wish tonight.
Bring true love into my life.

See? Simple. Right?

You've been casting spells out into the world all along. You just didn't know it.

You've got this. I know you do. Now, all you have to do is try.

And remember to keep it simple.

* * *

A Warning About Binding Spells:

Binding spells that one person casts upon another, are frequently done without the other person knowing.

Often, these spells are desperate attempts to salvage a floundering relationship, or prevent someone from leaving.

In a sense, these spells assert romantic ownership of one person by another.

These spells are often cast upon someone with very bad intentions. And once cast, spells of this nature rarely bring happiness or joy to either party.

* * *

Create a Magic Mirror

This spell creates a portable Magic Mirror. Any small compact mirror or hand held dresser mirror will work.

1. Hold the mirror in your left hand. Watch the full moon rise in the mirror's reflection. In your imagination, focus all of your energy on the smiling face of your heart's desire. (Fifteen to twenty minutes is long enough) This is where having a

photograph of your intended heart's desire is most helpful.

2. Place the mirror under your pillow or on your nightstand before you go to sleep.

3. When you wake up you will be the proud owner of a very potent love charm. To use it: Hold the mirror in your left hand, and capture the reflection of your heart's desire (by focusing the mirror over your shoulder) inside your magic mirror. Then, focus on all of your most positive feelings about your heart's desire into your magic mirror. Let those positive feelings steer your heart's desire in your direction. But be very careful. Whoever glances into your mirror while you are looking at them, will fall in love with you.

4. Replenish the mirror's magic by repeating step one on the next full moon.

* * *

How to Make Instant Attraction Oil

Needed:

Grated lemon zest

Two drops lavender essential oil

Three drops vanilla essential oil

Sweet almond oil

Directions:

1. Grind the dried lemon zest to a fine powder.

2. Place the powdered zest in the bottom of a glass bottle.

3. Add two ounces of sweet almond oil.

4. Add the essential oils drop by drop.

5. Cap the bottle and shake well.

Warning: Always remember to keep your imagery positive!

* * *

How To Make Rose Water

1. Place a rose (without the leaves and stem, just use the flower head) in a dish with enough water to cover the flower.

2. Wait for the flower to unfold. This may take 2 to 3 days or perhaps longer.

3. Change the water in the dish daily, and save this water in a container for magical use.

* * *

How to Make Mermaid's Amore (Love) Oil

1. Place a small seashell, a piece of coral (or a coral bead), and a single fresh rose petal inside a small glass bottle.

2. Cover these items with sweet almond oil (You can substitute coconut, olive, or baby oil).

3. Add a few drops of lavender essential oil to the bottle.

4. Add a pinch of cinnamon.

5. Cork the bottle to seal it tightly closed, and shake the contents to mix well.

6. To activate the magic in the oil, place the bottle on a windowsill so the oil will be bathed in the moonbeams from a full moon.

* * *

How to Reverse or Stop a Spell Gone Horribly Wrong

Note to the Spell Caster: Use this spell to take back any spell you regret casting.

Reasons to reverse a spell:

1. Undesirable results.

2. The spell is no longer needed.

Needed: What do you have left over from the original spell? Is there a paper doll, a swatch of fabric, or a charm bag of rose petals hidden in your jewelry box, or perhaps tucked away in a Magic Spell Box in the back of an underwear drawer, or under your bed?

Here are a few different ways to reverse a spell:

Burn or cut up the remnants (the left over pieces of paper, fabric)

Redirect the spell: Recast the original spell in a direction, or on a target that can't be harmed. A paper doll substituted for the original target works well here.

To temporarily pause a spell, place your spell-casting remnant, (paper doll, folded charm, etc.) in the freezer.

2

Candle Spells

Heart's Desire Candle Spell
(The spell to use when you know who you want.)

Use this spell to persuade your heart's desire to return your affections.

Needed: 3 candles: 2 pink or red tapered candles, and one white pillar candle.

2 candlestick holders and one flameproof plate.

Note: The first candle (a taper) represents you, the second (also a taper) represents your heart's desire, and the third candle (the pillar) increases the chances of romance between the first and second candles.

Directions:

1. Carve your first name into one of the tapers. Carve the first name of your heart's desire into the second taper.

2. Arrange the two tapered candles so they are six inches apart.

3. Place the third candle, below and between the two red or pink tapers, to form a triangle.

4. Dress the candles with Instant Attraction Oil. (dress means to rub a tiny bit of the oil on the sides of the candle)

5. Focus your intentions and all your positive thoughts on your heart's desire.

6. Speak your wish.

7. Light the candles.

8. Let your candles burn for 5 minutes, then extinguish.

P.S. This spell works great on the night of a new moon.

* * *

Halloween Love Spell

Needed:

Small piece of white paper

One red candle

Pen

Directions:

1. Write your most deeply felt romantic affirmations and aspirations on the single piece of white paper.

2. Fold the paper toward you, forming it into a neat package and seal it closed with wax dripped from the red candle.

3. Toss the sealed paper into a fire on Halloween Night.

Warning: This spell is extremely powerful when Halloween falls on the night of a full moon.

* * *

Candle Love Spell

Needed:

   Pink candle

   Rose petals

   Flameproof plate

   Directions:

   1. Sprinkle the petals around your candleholder (or plate).

   2. Place your candle on your candleholder.

   3. Light your candle.

   4. Repeat the spell three times.

   5. Focus on the flicking flame for 30 minutes while thinking about what true love means to you.

Spell:

I wish I may,

I wish it to last.

I wish for true love,

To find me fast.

Extinguish your candle.

* * *

Flame of Love Spell

Needed:

White pillar candle
Flameproof dish
Directions:
1. Place your candle on the flameproof dish, and light the wick.
2. Think about your heart's desire.
3. Repeat the spell.

Spell:

Flame of love flickering bright,
Aid me in my quest tonight.
Bring my true love straight to me,
As I will it, so shall it be.

When finished, extinguish your candle.

* * *

Group Gossip Banishing Spell

(Use this spell when gossip about you is coming from a group of people.)

Needed:
Small piece of white fabric
Marker
Black yarn or thread
Sewing needle or yarn needle
White pillar candle

Flameproof plate

Directions:

1. Light your candle.

2. Using the marker, draw the faces of those involved in the gossip on the fabric. No great detail is needed. Simply include one identifying feature (like eye glasses, earrings, or freckles).

3. Write the names of the people involved beneath each drawing.

4. Thread your needle, and then stitch over each mouth in your drawing.

5. While sewing the mouths closed, keep repeating the spell until you are finished.

Spell:

Your rumors are foul,
And much trouble they cause.
My stitches are tight,
And make your words pause.
When kindness and caring change your way,
Your speech will return without delay.

Note: When finished, extinguish your candle. Fold up the fabric and put it in a safe place.

* * *

Pearls of True Love, Candle Love Spell

Needed:

White candle
Flameproof plate
Swatch of white fabric
3 Pearls (or white plastic beads)
Glass bowl, the bigger the better
Silver-colored spoon
A small fabric pouch, preferably red
Directions:

1. Lay your fabric out on a smooth surface.

2. Place your bowl in the center of your fabric swatch and fill with clean water.

3. Light the candle and place it on your flameproof plate next to your fabric swatch.

4. Hold the pearls tightly in your hand.

5. Recite the spell.

6. Drop one pearl into the water, let it settle to the bottom, and turn around until you are once again facing the bowl.

7. Repeat the spell.

8. Drop your second pearl into the water, let it settle to the bottom, and again, turn around until you are facing the bowl.

9. Repeat the spell for a third time, drop the last pearl into the water, and make your final turn.

Spell:

By the power of fire,
By the power of light.
By the power of water,
And all that is right.
Let my love come to me.
Let him (or her) be true.

10. Finally, using your spoon, take a tiny sip of water from the bowl.

11. Repeat the spell above for a fourth and final time.

12. Leave the bowl where it is until all the water has evaporated.

The larger the bowl, the more powerful, and quicker will be your results.

When finished, extinguish your candle.

Later, after the water has evaporated, place the pearls in the pouch and carry them with you. Preferably in a pocket close to your heart.

* * *

Love and Friendship Attraction Spell

Needed:

Pink or white bed sheets

Three white or pink floating votives (these are flameless floating candles)

A handful of sea salt or other bath salts you have on hand

Music in line with achieving your desired result (love and friendship songs)

Directions:

1. Cover your mirrors with the sheets.

2. Draw a bath and add a handful of your chosen salts to the

water.

3. Switch on the three votive candles and set them afloat in the bathtub.

4. Relax and focus on the things you like about yourself. If you are casting this spell to attract your heart's desire, think about him or her.

5. Turn off the lights.

6. Turn on your favorite music.

7. Say the spell as you enter the tub.

Spell:

Negativity is washed away.
I am renewed as of today.
May many a head turn my way.
But, the one(s) I choose will wish to stay.

8. Soak In the bath and relax as long as you wish.

9. When finished, repeat the spell, exit the tub, and then make yourself a refreshing cup of herbal tea.

* * *

Love Attraction Charm

Needed:
   Rose Petals
   Sheet of Red Paper
   White Candle
   Flameproof plate

Directions:

1. Lay the paper on a flat surface.

2. Place the rose petals in the center.

3. Fold the paper over 5 times, to form an envelope around the petals inside.

4. Seal the folded paper closed with a few drops of wax dripped from the candle.

5. Draw a heart on the outside of your folded paper.

6. Carry this love charm in your pocket to attract love.

When finished, extinguish your candle.

* * *

Make Anyone Fall In Love With You

Needed:

Small pink candle

Pink or red construction paper

Scissors

Flameproof saucer

Pinch of ground cinnamon

Rose petals

Directions:

1. Cut a paper doll out of your construction paper.

2. Light your candle and place it on your flameproof plate.

3. Write your wishes, desires, and goals on the back of your paper doll.

4. Write the name of your heart's desire on the front of your

paper doll.

5. Write your name over your heart's desires' name three times.

6. Place your paper doll on the saucer.

7. Sprinkle the doll with rose petals and cinnamon.

8. Place your candle on top of your doll.

9. Light your candle while focusing your thoughts on your heart's desire.

10. Let your candle burn out.

Peel your paper doll away from the solidified candle wax.

Put your doll in a safe place.

* * *

Perfect Storm Candle Love Spell
Or
The Love Spell for Right Now

Needed:

One red candle

Vanilla extract

A few drops of Tabasco Sauce

3 whole cloves

Flameproof plate

Directions:

1. Recite the spell as you rub vanilla extract on the candle. (This is called dressing or anointing the candle).

2. Push the 3 cloves into the candle along the same side.

3. Rub the bottom of the candle with Tabasco sauce.

4. Place the prepared candle on a flameproof plate and light.

Spell:

Ignite the wick.
Fan the flame.
Grow a passion,
Hard to tame.

5. Repeat the spell four times more (for a total of 5) while the candle burns.

6. Visualize the person you desire getting warmed by the flame.

7. Repeat this spell for a sixth and final time after you finish visualizing.

When finished, extinguish your candle.

3

Remember Paper Dolls?

Love Attraction Spell:

1. Write the name of your heart's desire on a small piece of paper.

2. Sprinkle it with the most fragrant fresh flower petals you can get your hands on. My personal favorites include roses, gardenias, lilacs, honeysuckle, and orange blossoms.

3. Fold the paper toward you, forming it into a neat package.

4. Hide it in your underwear drawer to magically lure your heart's desire your way.

* * *

Origami Love Charm

Needed:
  Length of yarn (red or pink)
  Pen

Piece of paper (red, white, or pink)

Pinch of lavender

Directions:

1. Write your name and the name of your heart's desire in the center of your paper.

2. Sprinkle the pinch of lavender over the names.

3. Fold the paper over and over into a small tight packet being sure to keep the lavender inside.

4. Tie the packet closed with your length of yarn.

5. Carry this origami love charm with you to attract your heart's desire.

* * *

Paper Doll Chain Friendship Spell

Needed:

Piece of white or pink paper, 8 1/2" X 11"

Scissors

Tape

Pen

Directions:

1. Fold your paper In half lengthwise, so it is 4-1/2" wide and 11" long.

2. Cut paper along the fold.

3. Tape the two long pieces together so you have a piece of paper that is now 22" long and 4 1/2" wide.

4. Make a fold In your long piece of paper every 2", accordion-style.

5. Draw a figure of a person on top of your folded paper. Be sure the arms of your figure extend beyond your folded edges so your dolls, when unfolded will join.

6. Cut out the figure and unfold.

7. Write your name on the first doll.

8. Write the names of those people you wish to have as your friends on the other dolls.

9. Recite the spell as you fold your dolls together. Make sure to fold the doll with you name on it into the center of all of the dolls.

Spell:

A trusted and loyal friend I shall be to you.

My wish is for you to be that kind of friend to me, too.

Place your folded dolls In a safe place where they will remain undisturbed.

* * *

Paper Doll Love Enchantment

Needed:

Red candle

Length of red ribbon or yarn

Boy paper doll

Girl paper doll

Flameproof dish

Directions:

23

1. Light the candle.

2. While thinking about your heart's desire, fold the two paper dolls together and tie them with the ribbon or yarn.

3. Put the paper dolls in a safe place.

4. Extinguish the candle.

Pay absolutely no attention to your heart's desire.

Soon your heart's desire will display a strong interest in you.

* * *

Paper Doll Love Spell

Needed:

Single sheet of white, pink, or red paper

Pen

Scissors

Tape

Directions:

1. Fold your sheet of paper In half, from top to bottom.

2. Cut the paper in half along the fold.

3. Fold these two half sheets in half again.

4. Using the pen, along the fold of one half sheet draw a figure of half of a girl.

5. Along the fold of the second half sheet draw a figure of half of a boy.

6. With your scissors, cut out your paper dolls and unfold.

7. Tape the dolls together at the hands.

Note: If you are uncertain about how to draw your dolls before cutting them out, Google the words "making paper dolls".

8. Write you name on one paper doll.

9. Write the name of your heart's desire on the other doll.

10. As you are folding your two dolls together, recite the spell.

Spell:

The love in my heart for you is true.
My deepest wish is for you to love me, too.

Place your folded dolls in a safe place, like a jewelry box, or your Magic Spell Box.

* * *

Photo Love Charm

Needed:

Small photograph
Length of wide red ribbon
Scissors
Directions:

1. Make a copy of a small photo of your heart's desire (a school picture is perfect for this). Save the original photo to use again.

2. Wrap the picture up, covering it completely in a red ribbon.

3. Keep it in a safe place as a love charm.

* * *

Heart's Desire Written Heart Spell

Needed:

Sheet of red paper

Pen or pencil

Directions:

1. Write the name of your heart's desire seven times on the sheet of red paper.

2. Draw a heart around these names by writing your own name in cursive. Do this without picking up the pen or pencil. You can lengthen each letter of your name as you write. Or, write your name repeatedly. The key to this spell is to keep the tip of your pen or pencil on the page until all seven of your heart's desire's names are completely enclosed inside your own.

3. As you are writing your name, chant these words out loud: "You are in my heart."

4. Fold the paper toward you seven times.

5. Keep this talisman in a safe place. Like your jewelry box, tucked within the pages of your diary, or hidden away in your Magic Spell Box.

P.S. Should your feelings change about this person, tear up the paper. By ripping through the heart, you break this spell, and remove the magic.

* * *

Bonus Paper Money Spell

Needed:

One piece of white paper

Pen

Directions:

1. On the paper, draw a $1, $5, $10, $20, $50, or $100 on it.

2. Fold the paper small enough to fit into your wallet or pocket.

3. Recite the spell three times.

Spell:

Money, money come to me,
As I say three times three.
As I close my eye and visualize
The money coming to me in many ways.
Money, money come to me,
As I say three times three.

4. Place the folded paper in your wallet and leave it there for nine days. Watch the money start coming to you.

5. Repeat this spell every nine days. Pay attention to how the money comes your way.

* * *

Someone Special Shoe Spell

Needed:

Sheet of red construction paper

Pen

Scissors

Directions:

1. Cut a heart from a piece of red construction paper.
2. Write the name of your heart's desire on the heart.
3. Wear the heart inside your shoe.

Note: Your heart's desire should soon approach you, allowing you the opportunity to make a favorable impression.

* * *

Soul Mate Spell

Needed:

Paper

Pen

Small heart shaped box, or a small box you've decorated with hearts

Directions:

1. Think about those qualities you most desire in a soul mate.
2. Write those qualities down on the paper.

Spell:

Send to me my perfect match.

Someone these words are meant to match.

A perfect love who is here for me.

Shall find his (or her) way home to me.

3. Recite the spell.

4. Fold the paper and place it in your heart box.

5. Place the box in a safe place where it will remain undisturbed.

6. Let nature take its course and allow destiny to draw your soul mate to you.

WARNING: DO NOT cast this spell if you are only interested in drawing someone to you for the prom or homecoming. You must be prepared to receive a very special love into your life.

* * *

Two Hearts Together Love Charm

Needed:

Sheet of red or pink construction paper

Rose petals

Sewing needle

Red thread

Pen

Scissors

Directions:

1. Cut two hearts from the same piece of red or pink construction paper.

2. Write your name on one. Write the name of your heart's desire on the other.

3. Sandwich the rose petals between the two hearts by placing them together so the names are facing the inside of this package.

4. With the needle and red thread, carefully sew the two paper hearts together.

5. Carry this love charm near your heart.

4

Talismans, Charms, & Locket Magic

Love Talismans

F airy tales are full of magic objects that draw love and good fortune to their owners.

What fairy tales always fail to mention is you can easily craft your own.

Most of what you need can be found around your house. Look for the items in the spice rack, a sewing box, box of fabric scraps, a desk drawer, or kitchen junk drawer.

The dollar store is also a wonderful place to search for hidden treasures you can craft into amulets and charms.

* * *

Conjure Bag Binding Spell

Use a conjure bag to bind your heart's desire to you.

Needed:

Sheet of red paper

Pen

Mermaid Amore Oil

Red fabric bag

Copy of photo of your heart's desire or a photo of both of you

Small piece of rose quartz

Directions:

1. Cut a heart from the sheet of red paper.

2. Write both of your names inside the heart.

3. Anoint (just put a couple of dabs on the heart with your finger) the heart with a drop of Mermaid Amore Oil.

4. Place the heart inside a red fabric bag.

5. Add the photo of your heart's desire, or the photo of the two of you together and happy, to the bag.

6. Add a piece of rose quartz and seven fresh rose petals.

7. Keep this bag beneath your mattress.

* * *

Key to the Heart Love Spell

Needed:

One found key

Directions:

1. Find a key. Pick it up.

2. As you pick up the key, call out the name of your heart's desire three times.

3. The person will be yours.

4. Keep the key in a safe place.

A jewelry box or your Magic Spell Box is always a great place to keep your amulets and charms.

* * *

Make a Love Attracting Charm Bag

Needed:

Scrap of red fabric

Scissors

Needle

Red thread

Piece of rose quartz

Three fresh rose petals

Directions:

1. Snip two 3" squares from a scrap of red fabric. Preferably flannel or felt, but any red fabric will do.

2. Sew up three of the sides.

3. Fill this fabric bag with a heart charm, a piece of rose quartz, and three fresh rose petals.

4. Sew up the remaining side.

5. Carry this love attracting charm bag near your heart to attract love.

* * *

Love Treasure Chest

Needed:
   Small Box
   Rose Petals
   Vanilla Bean
   Cinnamon Stick
   Sheet of white paper
   Piece of Rose Quartz

Directions:

1. Place the rose petals, the vanilla bean, cinnamon stick, and piece of rose quartz inside your box.

2. On the paper, write five qualities you would like your new love to possess. Personality traits like kindness, generosity, sense of humor, thoughtful, devoted, and supportive, are what you're looking for here.

3. Fold the paper in half and place it inside the box.

Each night, before bedtime, open the box and inhale the aroma. This will remind you of your search for love, and the scents will sweeten your dreams.

* * *

Locket Magic

A locket worn around the neck actually can serve as an elegant charm bag. The chain binds the spell.

Needed:

Locket

Small photo of your heart's desire

Strand of your hair

A single clove

Directions:

1. Focus all of your energy on your heart's desire.

2. Place a photo of your heart's desire inside a locket, together with a strand of your hair and a single clove.

3. Wear your locket often. Think of your heart's desire every time you touch the locket.

* * *

Mermaid's Charm Bag

Very few can resist the seductive power of a mermaid.

Needed:

Red flannel or red felt bag

Mermaid charm (your can draw one on a piece of paper if needed)

Seven fresh rose petals

Seven small seashells

Pinch of rosemary

Directions:

1. Place your mermaid charm in the red flannel or felt bag.

2. To this bag add seven fresh rose petals and seven small seashells.

3. Add a pinch of rosemary, and then stitch the bag shut.

4. Carry the bag with you to attract your heart's desire.

* * *

Magic Love-Attracting Ring

Needed:

Ring

Glass

Rose water

2 bay leaves

Felt tip marker

A new moon

Length of red ribbon or cord

Directions:

1. Collect your materials and have them ready on the night of the new moon.

2. Find or purchase a ring. A simple gold band, a class ring, or a signet ring will do just fine.

3. To charge the ring: Drop the ring in a glass filled with rose water.

4. Next you'll need the two bay leaves. Write your name on one, and the name of your heart's desire on the other.

5. Add the bay leaves to the glass containing the ring and the rose water.

6. To activate the magic in the ring, place the glass on a windowsill so it will be bathed in the moonbeams from the new moon to the full moon.

7. By the light of the full moon, remove the ring from the glass of rose water. Hold it near your heart and speak your heart's desire's name aloud.

8. Wear the ring on a red cord or ribbon around your neck, or on any finger.

9. Twist the ring on your finger three times to attract your heart's desire.

* * *

How to Create a Rose Quartz Dreams About You, Heart's Desire Love Charm

Needed:
   Any Thursday night
   Sheet of white paper
   Pen
   Piece of rose quartz
   Small piece of red fabric
   Directions:

1. On any Thursday night, write a list of the qualities you most desire most in your heart's desire. Or, simply visualize and name a specific person. (This is where yearbooks, school photos, and cell phone pictures come in real handy.).

2. Before you go to sleep for the night place a piece of rose quartz (preferably in the shape of a heart, if you can find one)

next to your bed, or under your pillow.

3. On Friday morning, the first thing you do after you wake up, and before you brush your teeth, grab that piece of rose quartz in your right hand. Then, hold it over your heart.

4. Close your eyes. Visualize your heart's desire in your mind. This will take some practice, so be patient with yourself as you teach your mind how to do this. Make the image of your heart's desire as real as possible. Take your time.

5. Kiss the rose quartz and wrap it up in the small piece of red fabric, folding it toward you as you wrap.

6. Keep this talisman with you for seven days. Carry it near your heart during the day. Sleep with it at night, under your pillow, or next to you on your nightstand.

7. Repeat the visualization process every morning. After seven days you will have created a very powerful love-attracting amulet.

* * *

Rose Quartz Love Talisman

Rose quartz attracts your heart's desire in your direction.

Wear this semiprecious gemstone as jewelry, or carry it with you in a red fabric charm bag.

5

Mirrors & Ribbons, Wish Bottles & Knots

Wish Bottles 101

A wish bottle is a small charm or talisman used for bringing love, affection, happiness, and beauty your way, rather than ensnaring any one person in particular.

When selecting a wish bottle consider the way your vial looks, as well as what you intend to put in it.

For example: You might want to select a red vial for love, a blue one for beauty, a yellow one for happiness, or a green one for affection.

Get it?

* * *

Wish Bottle Spells

Needed:

One empty perfume bottle or small vial with a cork or stopper.

Directions:

1. Pull the stopper from your bottle as you think about your wish.

2. Meditate on your wish for a few moments. In your imagination, see what you want to happen.

3. Whisper your wish into the bottle.

4. Place the stopper back in the bottle, trapping your wish inside.

Once your wish bottle is closed, don't open it again until your wish comes true.

Put your bottle in a place that makes sense to you, where you will see it often, and it will remind you of your wish.

For example: If your wish is to attract new love, and they have your phone number, keep your wish bottle near your phone.

* * *

Magic Mirror Binding Spell

Needed:

Ginger bread dough (any cookie dough or play dough will do, but ginger bread is best)

Large heart-shaped cookie cutter

Small mirror

Oven (have your mom supervise)

Glue

Sequins, beads, or glitter

Red silk or flannel fabric

Directions:

1. Cut ginger bread (ginger bread is the longest lasting and most durable of all cookie dough) dough with a large heart-shaped cookie cutter.

2. Push a small mirror into the center of your cookie.

3. Bake in a low, slow oven.

4. When cooled, decorate your cookie with red beads, heart-shaped beads and sequins. Decorate your Magic Mirror Charm as fancy or as simple as you wish.

5. When ready, you and your heart's desire should gaze into the mirror together and promise your devotion to one another.

6. Wrap your mirror in a red silk or red flannel cloth, folding it toward you. Keep your mirror in a safe place.

7. Bring it out whenever your promise of devotion to one another needs to be strengthened.

* * *

Mend a Friendship Spell

Needed:

Large bowl (glass or ceramic). A large cereal bowl will work.

Pinch of salt

Key

Two foot length of pink ribbon or yarn

Water

Directions:

1. Tie the ribbon or yarn to the key.

2. Fill the bowl with water.

3. Add your pinch of salt and stir with your finger.

4. Dangle the key over the rippling water.

Spell:

Calm the waters with my friend.

I desire our troubles to come to an end.

5. Repeat this spell until the surface of the water in your bowl is completely still.

6. Wear the key around your neck for seven days.

7. Do your part to repair the damage to your broken friendship.

* * *

Reflect Away Harm Spell

(Good for dispelling rumors and meanness.)

Needed:

Two Small Mirrors

One White Candle

Flameproof dish

Knife

Directions:

1. Carve an X into the side of your candle.

2. Set up the mirrors so they face each other.

3. Place the candle on the flameproof plate between the two mirrors.

4. Light the candle. The candle flame should be reflected repeatedly, deep into the mirrors.

Spell:

May the harm intended upon me,
Be trapped here tonight.
Between these mirrors,
May it never again see the light.

5. Recite the spell

When finished, extinguish your candle.

* * *

Red Ribbon Love Spell

To find a bit of red ribbon, cord, string, yarn, or fabric indicates luck in love, and a change in romantic fortune is headed your way.

When you pick up the scrap, make a wish.

A request for love, luck, and happiness is best.

Carry the scrap with you as an amulet.

* * *

Spell Magic with Knots

Needed:

Full moon

Long piece of red or pink yarn, ribbon, or thread.

Directions:

1. By the light of a full moon, speak your wish.

2. Tie one knot into the strand as you recite each line of the spell below:

Spell:

By knot of one, the spell's begun.

By knot of two, it shall come true.

By knot of three, may it be.

By knot of four, this magic I store.

By knot of five, this spell's alive.

By knot of six, this spell I fix.

By knot of seven, events begin to leaven.

By knot of eight, it shall be fate.

By knot of nine, what's done is mine.

3. Seal your knotted thread in an envelope and place it where it will remain undisturbed.

* * *

Triple Knot Love Spell

Needed:

A 36" length of Red Ribbon

Your Favorite Perfume

Directions:

1. Place a few drops of your favorite perfume into the palm of your hand.

2. Rub your hands together.

3. Run your hands along the length of both sides of the ribbon.

4. Tie 3 knots evenly along the length of your ribbon, while reciting the spell.

Spell:

By knot one, my love will come.

By knot two, my love will be true.

By knot three, so shall it be.

Once you've completed this spell, store the ribbon in your Magic Spell Box.

* * *

Wish Bottle Love Charms

Needed:

Tiny bottle or vial with a cork or stopper

Pen

Small slip of red or pink paper

Directions:

1. Write the name of your heart's desire on the paper.

2. Roll the paper into a tight scroll and place it inside the wish bottle.

3. Whisper your wish into the bottle.

4. Place the cork into the wish bottle.

5. Store your wish bottle in a place, where upon seeing it, you will think about the wish you placed inside.

6. Upon seeing your wish bottle, meditate on your heart's desire.

Do not open your wish bottle again until your wish comes true.

6

More Candle Spells & One with Fire

Burn It Banishing Spell

Needed:
Small piece of paper
Pen
Fireproof bowl or foil pan on a heat protected surface
Matches or lighter
Have an adult handy to supervise
Directions:

1. Write down on the small piece of paper exactly what it is you wish to banish. Examples: A bad habit you wish to change like nail biting, negative self-talk, rumors and gossip, or the name of a person you want to leave you alone.

2. Focus on what you've written.

3. Light the piece paper on fire and drop it into the bowl or foil pan.

4. While the paper is burning, imagine what your life will be like when the banishing occurs.

5. Dispose of the ashes after they have thoroughly cooled.

Scatter them to the wind, or place them in an outside trashcan.

Make sure when you dispose of the ashes, to get them as far away from you as you can.

* * *

Gossip Banishing Spell
When you want the person spreading the gossip to stop!

Needed:

Small square of white fabric (a handkerchief will do)

Felt tip marker

Black yarn or thread

Sewing needle or yarn needle

White candle

Flameproof dish

Directions:

1. Light your candle.

2. With the marker, draw the face of your gossip on the fabric. The best way to do this is to tape the fabric to a piece of cardboard to keep the fabric flat while drawing. No need to go into great detail with your drawing. One or two identifying features like; glasses, dimples, pierced ears, or long or short hair is plenty.

3. Write the person's name under your drawing.

4. Thread your needle, then stitch over the mouth of your drawing, sewing the mouth shut.

5. While you are sewing the mouth shut, repeat the spell

below three times.

Spell:

Your words are lost,
No need to find.
Again you will talk,
When your words are kind.

When finished, extinguish your candle. Fold up the fabric and put it in a safe place.

After a day or two you will feel the gossiping has stopped.

* * *

Moonlight Candle Spell
(This is a protection spell.)

Needed:
  One white pillar candle
  Moonlight
Directions:
  1. Place the candle on your windowsill in the moonlight.
  2. While holding your hands over the candle, visualize the moonlight's powerful rays of protection being absorbed into the candle's wax.

Spell:
Charge this candle by my will.

Candle sitting on my windowsill.
Fill it with power.
Soak it with love,
And protection rays from up above.
From sun to moon, and moon to me,
Create this protection candle just for me.

3. Repeat this spell as many times as you feel are needed.
   4. Leave your unlit candle on the windowsill in the moonlight over night.

* * *

Quick & Easy Candle Spell

Needed:
   One candle (pink, red, or white)
   Flameproof dish
Directions:
1. Place candle on the flameproof dish and light.
2. Recite the spell below.

Spell:
As the candle burns and flames stretch higher,
May our passion catch fire.
Love and lust grow intertwined,
This is what I yearn to find.

When finished, extinguish your candle.

* * *

Reuniting Lost Love Spell

Needed:

Six candles in the following colors: 1 red, 1 green, 1 yellow, 1 blue, 2 pink.

Directions:

1. Place the candles at the appropriate compass points. Red - South. Green-North. Yellow-East. Blue-West.

2. Light all 6 candles.

3. Hold the two pink candles in your hands.

4. Face the red or south indicating candle.

5. Recite the spell.

Spell:

Magic, magic hear my plea.

If our love is meant to be,

Return [insert the name of your heart's desire here] back to me.

When finished, extinguish your candles.

* * *

Self-Love
&
Self-Confidence Spell

Before you are able to receive love from another, you must have the courage to love yourself first.

Roses stimulate and teach self-love, self-confidence, self-forgiveness, and self-acceptance.

Place a few fresh rose blossoms in a mesh bag and add the flowers to your bath water.

You can also place dried flower petals in a mesh bag and add those to your bath.

Surround yourself with small bouquets of wild flowers and living plants.

* * *

Simple Love Spell

Needed:
  White pillar candle
  Flameproof plate
  Directions:
  1. Light the candle.
  2. Recite the spell below.

Spell:
Magic moon a quarter bright,
Bring me what I ask tonight.

A little love is all I need,
I can do the rest in deed.
The one I love needs a tiny nudge,
Into my arms, where (s)he can't budge.
And there (s)he forever stays,
For the rest of our remaining days.

When finished, extinguish your candle.

* * *

Three Wishes Candle Spell

Needed:
   One candle, any color
   Flameproof dish
   Directions:
   1. Light the candle.
   2. Recite the spell below.

Spell:
Three wishes. Three fishes.
Grant my wishes.
I need a little cheat,
So make my wish come true.

When finished, extinguish your candle.

* * *

Wish Upon A Star True Love Spell

Needed:
Clear night when you are able to see the stars.
Pink candle
Flameproof plate
Directions:
1. Find the brightest star in the sky.
2. Light your candle and set it on the plate.
3. Recite the spell below seven times as you visualize your heart's desire in your imagination.

Spell:
Star light, star bright,
Brightest star in the sky tonight.
I wish I may, I wish I might,
With my true love, may I unite.

When finished, extinguish your candle.

* * *

Your Heart's Desire Name, Paper, Candle Spell

Needed:
Paper

Scissors

Pen

Small straight pin

Glass

Water

Few drops of honey

Red or pink pillar candle

Flameproof plate

Attraction Oil or Mermaid Amore Oil

Directions:

1. Cut two slips of paper about the same size of a fortune you'd find in a fortune cookie.

2. Write you name on one. Write the name of your heart's desire on the other.

3. Pin the two pieces of paper together in the form of a cross, with your name on top.

4. Place this paper cross in the glass containing water and honey.

5. Dress a red or pink candle with Attraction Oil or Mermaid Amore Oil. (Rub the oil on the sides of the candle)

6. Place the candle in front of the glass.

7. Light your candle for a few minutes each day for the next nine days.

When finished, extinguish your candle.

This spell is most powerful when you start burning your candle on the day of a new moon.

7

Flower Power & Stuff You Find Outside

Chains of Violets Love Spell

F ind a hearty violet plant.

Weave the flowers into long chains.

Hang the chains in your bedroom to attract your heart's desire.

* * *

Love Safety Spell

Do you suspect someone is attempting to enchant you?

A white lily (real or artificial) renders a woman immune to the effects of undesired love potions, charms, and spells.

* * *

Red Rose Spell

Needed:
   One long-stemmed red rose
   Two red taper candles
   Candlestick holders
   Mermaid Amore Oil or Instant Attraction Oil
   Directions:

1. Place the single long-stemmed red rose between the two red tapered candles.

2. Dress the candles with Mermaid Amore Oil or Instant Attraction Oil. By dressed, I mean just rub a little oil on the sides of your candles.

3. Burn your candles, leaving the rose in place between them.

4. Think about your heart's desire as the candles burn.

When finished, extinguish your candles.

* * *

Lookingfor a New Love?
Try this violet leaf spell.

Ever notice how violet leaves look like little hearts?

Place a couple of these leaves in your shoes to attract your heart's desire. Or, allow the leaves to guide you to the right match.

* * *

Snail Shell Charms

1. To win love, abandoned snail shells make the perfect love charms. Gently carry a snail shell on your body.

2. Give it to your heart's desire, and get him or her to carry it.

3. Beware: Snail shells are fragile. If the shell is crushed, take the time to determine if this is a sign this person is a poor match for you.

* * *

Talisman of Love: Earrings

Any earring with a red stone qualifies.

However, these particular stones contain more magic.

Coral Earrings

Garnet Earrings

Ruby Earrings

Wear a pair to attract your heart's desire.

* * *

Cherished One
Apple Spell

Share a single apple with your heart's desire to protect your love.

This spell keeps others from luring your beloved away.

P.S. This spell will work with a pear, too.

* * *

Romance Attracting Power of Beryl Gems

Beryl gemstones cement and solidify romance. They are also used to rescue and renew fading love.

These gems are most effective when worn as a ring or a necklace.

Wearing beryl gemstones also help you gain control over negative situations.

Stones in the Beryl Gem family include:

Topaz (yellow and blue)

Emerald

Morganite aka pink emerald

Aquamarine

Garnet

* * *

The Ruby

It is believed that rubies possess the power to increase energy levels and stimulate love when worn close to the heart.

They are also believed to:

Protect sensitive temperaments

Improve health

Increase wealth

Control passion

Stimulate circulation

Eliminate sleeplessness and nightmares

Reduce depression

Ward off evil spirits

* * *

Walnut Love Charm

Needed:

Sheet of red paper

Scissors

Attraction Oil or Mermaid Amore Oil

Pen

Empty walnut shell

Red candle

Flameproof plate

An old sock belonging to your heart's desire

Directions:

1. Cut a heart from the sheet of red paper.

2. Write the name of your heart's desire on the heart.

3. Place a single drop of Attraction Oil or Mermaid Amore Oil on his or her name.

4. Fold the heart toward you, making it into a tiny packet.

5. Place your folded heart inside an empty walnut shell.

6. Place the other half of the walnut shell on top and seal the two halves together with wax dripped from a red candle.

7. This charm should not be discovered. Place it somewhere your heart's desire won't find it.

8. Or, borrow an old used sock from your heart's desire, and slip the walnut inside it.

9. Make a knot in the sock, sealing your intention. Then hide the sock under your mattress.

When finished, extinguish your candle.

* * *

White Magic Love Charm

Needed:

Piece of rose quartz

Small silver-colored plate

Rose petals from a single red rose

New moon

Charm bag

This spell gets best results when performed on the night of a new moon, when there is no visible moon in the sky.

Directions:

1. Kiss the rose quartz crystal.
2. Set it on the plate.
3. Sprinkle the rose petals, covering the crystal.
4. Set the plate on a windowsill, in a place where you know the moonlight is sure to shine upon it, for the next seven days.
5. After the seven days have come and gone, place the rose quartz crystal in a charm bag and keep it with you. The crystal will draw love and romance into your life.
6. Leave the plate and petals on the windowsill until the next new moon.

Should a new love enter your life during this time, place the petals in an envelope and store them in a safe place. If no one captures your heart during this time, scatter the rose petals into the wind, and repeat this spell.

8

Complicated Spells

Attracting The Right Person Spell

A dd a few drops of Instant Attraction Oil to your bath every Friday night until you have found the love you desire.

Don't settle for just anyone to love you. You need the right person.

This spell is beneficial for a long-term love-of-your-life kind of search.

* * *

Binding Spell Using Dolls

Needed:
   Boy doll
   Girl doll

Outfits for each doll

Red or pink ribbon or yarn

Directions:

1. Obtain two dolls. Barbie and Ken work great, but Raggedy Ann and Andy work well, too. If you can't find any real dolls, make paper ones instead.

2. Focus your thoughts on your heart's desire as you dress and adorn your dolls with clothes, shoes, and jewelry. For example: Prom dress for Barbie. Tux for Ken.

3. Face the dolls toward each other. Tie them together using ribbon (or yarn), making knots as you work the ribbon up the dolls. Wrap from the feet, working your way up to the head.

4. Hide the dolls in a safe place, like a shoebox, for as long as you wish this romance to continue.

* * *

Footprint Binding Spell

(I got into a whole lot of trouble with this spell in Lilly Noble & the Secret Garden!)

Needed:

Small garden shovel

Baggie

Flowerpot

Marigold seeds

Directions:

1. Find a good footprint left behind by your heart's desire.

2. Place your foot beside his or her footprint, making a matching footprint. Meaning: If you have his left footprint, you make a footprint using your right foot.

3. Using a small garden shovel, carefully dig up both footprints, and place the dirt in a Baggie.

4. Put the dirt in a flowerpot.

5. Plant marigold seeds. Follow the directions on how to care for the seeds, and watch your love flourish.

I'd like to add a word of caution here. Make sure the footprint you dig up belongs to your heart's desire, and not someone else.

* * *

Heart's Desire Hair Spell

Obtain a lock of hair (or even a single strand will do) from your heart's desire. Wear it in your hat to turn their heart your way.

* * *

Heart's Desire Needle Love Charm

Needed:

  Two sewing needles

  Mermaid Amore Oil

Directions:

1. Take two needles.

2. Dress them with Mermaid Amore Oil.

3. Name one for yourself. Name the other one for you heart's desire.

4. Insert the point of your heart's desire's needle into the eye of your needle. However, to suit the purposes of a male preforming this spell, you'll need to adjust the needles.

5. Keep this love charm in a safe place where the needles will not get separated.

* * *

Transform Yourself Into a Mystic or Mystery

(We're similar to wizards & witches, but very different in strange and wonderful ways.)

Imagine a clan symbol. This symbol can be anything you choose. Examples: Heart, four-leaf clover, horseshoe, star, moon, mermaid, fleur de lis, clock, etc.

Needed:
Sheet of pink or red construction paper
Pen
Scissors
Directions:
1. Draw your symbol on your piece of paper.
2. Using the scissors, cut your drawing from the paper.
3. Hold your chosen symbol over your heart.

4. Chant the spell below three times.

Spell:
Powers of Actual Magic rise.
Soar my way across the sky.
Magic powers come to me.
I call you near.
Find me here.
And, settle in the heart of me.

5. Stash you symbol in a safe place, like your Magic Spell Box.

* * *

Make Clay for Crafting
Beads, Charms, and Amulets

Needed:
   3 cups Flour
   1 1/2 cups Salt
   1 1/2 cups Cornstarch
   Warm water
   Cookie cutters
   Toothpicks
   Acrylic paints
   Paint brushes or markers
   Glitter
   Clear acrylic spray varnish
   Rattail cord, lanyard cord, ribbon, yarn, or fishing line

Directions:

1. In a large bowl, mix dry ingredients together.

2. Add warm water by slowly adding it until the mixture becomes moist enough to be kneaded into dough. The dough should be firm and sticky enough to be rolled into bead-sized balls.

3. Roll the dough out flat with a rolling pin, or roll into bead-sized balls.

4. Cut small charms or amulet shapes into the dough, (bats, stars, moons, hearts, witches' hats) using a knife or cookie cutters.

5. Pierce your shapes and bead-sized balls with toothpicks, making holes large enough for later stringing.

6. Place your creations on a foil-lined cookie sheet and bake in the oven at 200 degrees for an hour and a half, or allow them to dry on the counter over night.

7. When the clay is cool and dry, paint your creations with acrylic paint, add some glitter, and string your pieces together. If you'd like to add a glossy finish, a quick spray of acrylic varnish will do the trick.

* * *

Rose Petal Love Beads

(Through the ages, all love beads have been crafted using fresh rose petals.)

Needed:

Petals from a dozen fresh red or pink roses

Food processor
Large darning needle
Heavy red or pink thread
Directions:

1. Chop a pile of fresh rose petals (just the rose petals, be sure to remove all the green bits of the stem and leaves) from the roses in a food processor. Or, using a mortar and pestle, grind them down. Do this until the petals form a fine paste.

2. Using your fingers, roll small amounts of your rose petal paste into beads. Make you beads no larger than a medium sized pearl. As you work with the rose petal paste, concentrate and visualize spending time with your heart's desire. Whisper your feelings of love as you roll each bead.

3. While your beads are still damp and pliable to the touch, pierce each one through the center with a large darning needle. These holes will allow you to string them together with a heavy thread later. Visualize your heart being pierced with Cupid's arrow as you pierce each bead.

4. Let your beads dry. Turn them frequent to make sure your beads dry on all sides.

5. When completely dry, (drying can take up to a week in some humid climates) string your beads on to a long piece of heavy thread.

6. Wear your strands of Rose Petal Love Beads, or hang them over your bed.

Word of warning: Do not allow the beads to get wet. They will disintegrate.

* * *

Wish Bone Love Spell

Needed:
  Wishbone
  Gold-colored acrylic paint
  Paintbrush
  Red charm bag
  Fresh petals from a red rose
  Directions:

You don't have to wait around until Thanksgiving to acquire a wishbone. These U-shaped bones are readily available all year round. Including turkeys, these delicate neck bones can also be found in whole game hens, whole chickens, pheasant, and ducks. Just be careful when removing your wishbone from your bird, as you need it to be in one piece for this spell.

1. After acquiring your wishbone, set it out for several days, allowing it to dry completely.

2. Paint your wishbone gold.

3. Carry your wishbone in a red charm bag along with the rose petals.

Recharge your wishbone from time to time by removing the old rose petals and adding fresh ones.

* * *

Wish Granting Spell

Needed:

Marking pen, like a Sharpie

Large leaf that has recently fallen from a tree.

A stone.

Directions:

1. Write the single word that represents the thing you want. Example: Love, money, job, marriage, boyfriend, prom, friend, etc.

2. Lay the leaf on the ground in a place where it will remain undisturbed.

3. Place your rock on top of the leaf.

As the leaf withers and decays, it will transport your desire into the earth.

In thanks, Mother Nature will grant your wish.

Note: You may also toss your leaf into rushing water, like a creek or river.

9

Easy Spells & Coin Spells

Keys to Casting Powerful Spells on the Fly

You don't have to buy a lot of weird tools to be a successful spell caster. If you want a wand, whittle one from a found stick. Some of the most powerful spells are hastily whispered incantations, simple symbols drawn on a scrape of paper, or thoughts envisioned and performed deep in the imagination.

The best time to cast a spell is when you are calm and relaxed.

All you need to do is think up a spell, and then jot down a short, quick incantation.

Here's one of my favorites.
Directions:
1. Find a bright star on a moonless night.
2. Think of something or someone you'd like to attract into your life.

3. Recite the spell below.

Spell:

Star light, star bright,
First star I see tonight.
I wish I may, I wish I might,
Have the wish I wish tonight.

* * *

Friendship Coin Charm

This friendship charm spell is really just a version of what I call love spell lite.

If you have a tendency to be on the shy side, use this charm to create a love relationship by creating a friendship first.

Needed:
Square of white fabric (a handkerchief works best).
Strand of pink ribbon or yarn.
Three coins (any coins will do)
Honeysuckle scent (perfume or oil)
Mint leaf (or a mint tea bag)
Directions:
1. Lay out the white cloth.
2. Place your mint leaf in the center.
3. Rub a drop of your honeysuckle scent on both sides of

each coin. You can use nickels, dimes, or quarters. The more valuable your coin, the more value is placed on the friendship you wish to attract.

4. Place the coins on top of the mint leaf.

5. Gather the fabric corners together.

6. Tie the fabric in a tidy bundle using your piece of pink ribbon or yarn.

Carry this friendship charm with you when you are out with people you would like to have for your friends.

* * *

Talisman of Love

Needed:

Chinese Coins

Square of red fabric

Traditional Chinese coins have square holes in the center. When you buy them, they are usually strung together with a red silk cord, for good luck and protection. (You can find them on Amazon)

Directions:

Wrap the coins in your square of red fabric. To bring the magic your way, make sure to fold the fabric toward you. Or, you can simply place the coins in a red fabric bag.

Wear this love charm near your heart.

* * *

Coin Charm

Needed:

Small envelope

Pinch of lavender

Coin (any coin will do, but one you find outside will produce the best results)

A couple of rose petals

Directions:

1. On the inside flap of the envelope write the name of your heart's desire, or simply write the words, *my heart's desire.*

2. Slip the lavender, the rose petals, and the coin into your envelope.

3. Seal the envelope closed with a kiss.

4. Place the envelope somewhere special, like your jewelry box or your Magic Spell Box.

* * *

Shimmering Silver Spell

Important note: Perform this spell on a cloudless night of a full moon.

Needed:

Ceramic bowl

Seven fresh basil leaves

Water (rain or spring)

Silver coin (a dime works well here, but the coin must have some silver in it)

Directions:

1. Place the coin in the bottom of your bowl.

2. Pour the water over the coin, filling the bowl only halfway.

3. Set the bowl in a window or on a table where the moonlight will shine on it.

4. Drop the basil leaves into the water, one by one while reciting the spell below.

Spell:

By the light of the moon,

Send blessings soon.

As silver in water shines bright,

May abundance and love be mine this night.

5. Leave your bowl in the moonlight until morning.

6. Pour the water and basil leaves into a corner of your yard where the basil leaves will remain undisturbed.

7. Carry the silver coin in your pocket.

* * *

Amas Amore Easy Love Spell

Needed:

A moonlit night

Directions:
Simply recite the spell below.

Spell:

Send the heart of the man (or woman) I seek.
Let him (her) know of no more peace,
Until the day (s)he comes to me.

* * *

Spell to Become Loving to Attract Love

Needed:
Moonlight
The truest desire to become a more loving person
Directions:
Recite the spell below, on moonlit nights, before going to sleep.

Spell:

To find new love and let it come in,
My words and deeds I must improve.
Words and actions both good and kind,
To which forever my true love shall bind.
Give me the love that love shall bring.
Change me forever, please do this thing.

* * *

Love Spell Chants

Here are three quick and easy spells requiring nothing at all, other than the spells themselves.

Love Spell #1:
By the power below and above,
Bring me someone to love.
With this spell I cast,
I want true love that will last.

Love Spell #2:
One, two, three, four,
Please reveal what's in store.
Five, six, seven, eight,
Bring the love that is my fate.

Love Spell #3:
Shadows and light,
Bring love to me tonight.
Light and shadow,
Send me a suitable beau.

* * *

Simple No Frills Love Spell

Needed:
  Moonlight

Recite the spell below.

Spell:
Grant to me this wish I make,
Of love to give and love to take.
Equal and fare,
Bring a great love for me to share.
Let it begin.

* * *

Yuletide Mistletoe Kissing Spell

According to ancient lore, and my great, great grandmother, Henrietta, a kiss under the mistletoe magically protects and preserves the love between those kissing beneath it. And, insures an enduring and everlasting relationship for the pair.

Here's something cool to think about. By keeping mistletoe hanging over your front door year round, you can repeat the kissing spell with your heart's desire as often as needed.

10

Spices & Herbs

Herbal Sachet Love Charm

Needed:
    Swatch of pink, red, or white fabric enough to make a small pouch
Needle & thread
1 Cinnamon stick
Pinch of Lavender
1 Vanilla bean
7 Whole cloves
7 Rose petals
Directions:
1. Gather your ingredients together.
2. Sew your swatch of fabric into a small pouch.
3. Tuck all the ingredients inside your pouch.
4. Stitch your pouch shut. Keep your stitches close to keep your ingredients inside your sachet charm pouch.
5. Place this Sachet Love Charm inside the pillowcase of your pillow.

After several nights of sleeping with your head on this sachet love charm, your dreams will connect with those of your heart's desire.

* * *

Grow Your Very Own Boyfriend Spell
(The heartier the plant, the better the boyfriend!)

Needed:
   Basil plants
   Directions:
   Grow Basil in several small pots and place them around your home.
   Fresh Basil plants attract love and happiness into you home.

* * *

Attract a New Love with Catnip

(Remember to put the cat out! When Grace performed this spell on Smuddy, Goliath practically stapled himself to the ceiling.)

Needed:
   Catnip
   Bowl

Rose water
Full moon
Strainer
Spray bottle
Directions:

1. Soak a teaspoon of catnip in small bowl of rose water overnight in the moonbeams of a full moon. [To make your own rose water, simply bring a pot of water and some rose petals to a boil. Turn off the heat, and allow the water to cool before removing the petals.]

2. Strain the catnip from the rose water.

3. Place this catnip charged rose water in a spray bottle.

4. For the next twenty-one days, spritz the liquid on your doorstep in the shape of a new crescent moon.

P.S. I made a crescent moon stencil from a piece of cardboard, to get the shape just right.

* * *

Bay Leaf Wish Spell

Needed:
Dried bay leaf
Felt tip marker
Directions:

1. Write your wish on a bay leaf. For example: Love.

2. Put your Bay leaf in a safe place, like a jewelry box, or your Magic Spell box.

* * *

Laurel Leaf Love Letter Spell

Needed:

New moon

Bay leaf

Red felt tip marker

Your favorite perfume

Red envelope

Directions:

1. On the evening of a new moon, write the name of your heart's desire on a bay leaf with a red marker.

2. Place a drop of your favorite perfume on the bay leaf.

3. Slip the bay leaf into the red envelope.

4. Sleep with the envelope under your pillow until the full moon.

5. Put the envelope in a safe place.

* * *

Key to Your Heart Love Spell

Needed:

Cinnamon stick

Key

3 Red candles

3 Flameproof plates

Directions:

1. Rub the cinnamon stick on the sides and top of your candle.

83

2. Place candles on flameproof dishes and light them.
3. Recite the spell below.

Spell:
May love draw you to me,
Like honey and a bee.
Then, use this key
To unlock me.

Place the key beneath your mattress directly below your heart. Once this spell attracts your new love, remove the key from beneath your mattress, and keep it in a safe place.

Be sure to extinguish the candles after reciting the spell.

* * *

Lemon Love Charm

Needed:
   Pinch of cinnamon
   Pinch of sugar
   One fresh lemon
   Small slip of paper (preferably pink or red, but white will do)
   Sharp knife
   Cutting board
   Yarn or ribbon (match the ribbon or yarn to your slip of paper, if possible)
   Directions:

1. On the paper, write your name and the name of your heart's desire. If you have no one special in mind, simply write *someone special*.

2. Fold the paper in half so the two names meet.

3. Slice the lemon open lengthwise.

4. Sprinkle the lemon halves with the cinnamon and sugar.

5. Sandwich the paper in between the lemon halves.

6. Use your length of ribbon or yarn to bind the lemon halves back together. Feel happiness as you visualize this new relationship.

7. Tuck your lemon in the back of your freezer.

While waiting for the arrival of your new love, joyously think about how the two of you will meet.

Note: If no new love appears in your life in 2-8 weeks, dispose of the lemon and try again.

* * *

No Strings Attached Love Spell

Looking for a prom date without the messy commitment?
Need a date to the dance?
Or for that special party?
This spell might help you fill that particular need.

Needed:
2 whole hot peppers

2 sticks of cinnamon incense

Flameproof plate or incense holder

Directions:

1. Light each stick of incense and place on opposite sides of your room.

2. Let them smolder for a few minutes to allow smoke to waft through the space.

3. Focus your thoughts on attracting someone who isn't interested in romance, but whose companionship you would find enjoyable for an evening or two.

4. Place the hot peppers under your pillow.

5. Sleep with the peppers under your pillow until the spell brings someone willing to fulfill your wish.

* * *

Love Bottle Spell

Needed:

White candle

Small bottle or jar with a stopper

2 found coins (same denomination: 2 pennies, 2 dimes)

2 cinnamon sticks

Petals from 2 red or pink roses

2 whole cloves

2 pinches of lavender

2 pinches of sugar

Directions:

1. Place everything into your bottle or jar.

2. Light your candle.

3. Carefully drip candle wax on to your cork or stopper.

4. While sealing the stopper into your container, chant the following spell three times.

Spell:

Coins, flowers, and spice
Send to me someone nice.

5. Extinguish your candle.

6. Store your bottle or jar in a safe place.

* * *

And finally, Love Spell #101

Star Love Spell
(Similar to the previous Flame of Love Spell.)

Note: This is an example of how you can switch up any spell when you don't have a candle handy.

Needed:
Bright star in the night sky
Directions:
Recite the spell below as often as you wish.

Spell:

Star of love burning so bright,
Aid me in my spell tonight.

Unite my true love straight to me,
As I will it, so shall it be.

11

Conclusion

To achieve success, you must do your part.

Magic spells don't create miracles all by themselves. You must perform your part as well.

Casting a love spell only to turn around and treat your heart's desire badly, well let's just say, that energy will come back to haunt you. Usually in the form of reputation damaging gossip and rumors.

A FINAL WORD OF CAUTION:

If your desire is to cast spells to get revenge or reek havoc in the life of another, my suggestion is for you to just let go your anger. And, move on.

Biography on Madam Saboulia By Shellaire Lombard

Madam Lucrezia Saboulia's background, education, and merit awards:

Background:

Okay so, no one really knows of Madam Saboulia's origins except of course, Madam Saboulia. She's probably very old, (I know this from stuff she says in class) and if you've ever laid eyes on her, well you'd know immediately that she's not from here. Meaning, you know, Earth. I asked her once to tell me about her childhood, and she wouldn't share a thing. So let's just say Madam Saboulia is likely from everywhere, and maybe nowhere.

Education, Merits, & Awards:

Universally respected (and probably feared!!!) shape-shifter.

Won the Bonaventure-Mondragon Competition for a powerful brat banishing potion while attending Bonaventure's Academy of Magic as a minor high school student (year unknown)

Graduated from Bonaventure's Academy of Magic with high honors (year unknown)

Graduated from the University of Dark Magic, Raven's Landing, Maine, with high honors (year unknown)

Magna Cum Laude Graduate from the University of Transylvanian Magic in Cluj, Romania (Founded in the year 1492 AD)

Thrice awarded The Eastern Order of the Golden Glinda, Good Witch Seal of Approval:

For her experiments proving kindness is rewarded, and evil punished

For her ability to shape-shift into random creatures in perilous moments

For her independent studies proving the safety of long term invisibility & walking through walls

TED Talks:

A Mystery's Advice for Curiosity-Driven Cats

How What You Think Shapes Your Magic

Being Respectful Prevents The Wicked Voodoo Curse

Zombies: The New Breed of White Walker

Books by Madam Lucrezia Saboulia:

The Cardiac Effect: Why Love Spells Are Good for Your Heart & Blood Pressure

Spells and Potions and Charms, oh my!

Boomerang Magic

Why Vampires Make Quiet Neighbors: Don't Bleed Where They Can Get a Whiff

Lucrezia Saboulia currently serves as Vice Chancellor and Dean of Girls at Bonaventure's Academy of Magic, where she also teaches Power of Intentions, Translation and Meaning of Ancient Runes & Egyptian Hieroglyphs, and Ethics in Magic.

FROM THE OWNER OF THE DIARY

Shellaire Guinevere Lombard, the winner of several local beauty pageants, was born to parents, Violet and Thane Lombard, in the coastal town of Sleepy Hollow, California, on May 9. A graduate of Twilight Elementary for the Gifted, and Sleepy Hollow Junior High (go Chargers!), Miss Lombard is currently enrolled at Bonaventure's Academy of Magic, located on Raven's Landing Island, Maine. The winner of the prestigious Bonaventure-Mondragon Competition, her entry: *How to Increase Your Wardrobe With Spells and Enchantments* has turned the world of fashion magic upside down.

Upon graduation from Bonaventure's Academy of Magic, Miss Lombard plans to attend the University of Dark Magic, also located on Raven's Landing Island. Postgraduate studies at University of Diplomatic Magic in London, England, will bring her closer to achieving her goal of becoming an Ambassador of Actual Magic to the World.

Her interest in love spells began shortly after a slumber party she attended while in the fifth grade. The desire to have a boyfriend, now finds Shellaire hard at work honing her skills in love spells, mystical amulets, and not too unpleasant potions.

Okay, she hasn't enchanted a boyfriend yet, so there's that. But she's been working on a very cool boyfriend-binding spell. So, you know, hopefully she'll have a real live boyfriend sometime soon.

A Note From The Author:

If you've enjoyed reading and casting these wonderful love spells,

A MYSTERY'S COLLECTION

OF

101 LOVE SPELLS

From the diary of SHELLAIRE LOMBARD

And the Magical World of Lilly Noble

please click on the book title. You will be taken to my book's Amazon page where you can leave a review. You will find stars to record your rating, and title and text boxes to enter your review and heading. When you're finished, click on the submit button is near the bottom of the book's page to enter your review and complete the process.

Also, find me on goodreads and join the fun!

Many thanks!
Deb

WANT TO KNOW WHAT'S HAPPENING ON RAVEN'S LANDING?

FOR UPDATES in the Lilly Noble series,
and Lilly & her friends,
enroll in Bonaventure's Academy of Magic
on Deborah's website at:
www.deborahmctiernan.com
And receive your
FREE Bonaventure's Academy Coat-of-Arms
iron on transfer for enrolling!
Don't forget to check out the merchandise in the
Bonaventure's Academy Gift Shoppe
while you're there!

About the Author

On July 4, in Philadelphia Pennsylvania, Deborah McTiernan was born into a family of avid readers. At the age of 4, she spent hours in her grandmother's attic typing on a portable, baby-blue Smith-Corona typewriter she discovered in an old steamer trunk. While pretending to write exciting stories of magical heroes and heroines, the keys of the typewriter ignited her imagination.

Her family was transferred from the East Coast to the Midwest. They eventually left the city and settled in a small rural community of Orion, Illinois (thinly disguised as Archer's Bow, Illinois in her story). It was while living in Orion at Deborah became a life-long fan of fairytales, myth, and magic. Summers off from school gave her plenty of time to haunt the town library, read her favorite stories on the front porch, and hone her skills as a storyteller.

Her *Lilly Noble* series is a pleasant new twist to the beloved and enduring fairy-tale genre, and in the hands of this author, this is just the beginning.

Deborah Lives in Arizona.

You can connect with me on:

🌐 https://www.deborahmctiernan.com
🐦 https://twitter.com/Deb_McTiernan
📘 https://www.facebook.com/deborah.tirneymctiernan
🔗 https://www.deborahmctiernan.com/shop

Subscribe to my newsletter:

✉️ https://www.deborahmctiernan.com/contact

Also by Deborah McTiernan

Lilly Noble & Actual Magic
Book One

Lilly Noble & Actual Magic, a gremoire
The Companion Journal

Lilly Noble & the Phantom Rush
Book Two

Lilly Noble & the Secret Garden
Book Three

A Mystery's Collection of 101 Love Spells,
   From the Diary of Shellaire Lombard
   And the Magical World of Lilly Noble
   The Companion Novel to
   Lilly Noble & the Secret Garden

Deb's TOP SECRET CONFIDENTIAL
   Storyteller Workbook